ABNER'S CABIN

by ALF EVERS

Illustrated by LEONARD WEISGARD

Abner rode through the forest and found just the place to build a home for his children. He cut down logs and built a cabin with four walls and a roof and a door. When he and his wife died, after tilling the fields and bringing up a family, there was another family, and another, and each one added or built on the original cabin. One day a man wanted to tear it down to build a filling station and instead created a museum out of the original Abner's cabin. The people of Abnersville learned how there came to be a town and how people worked and lived many years ago and felt great pride in accomplishment.

* *

Dewey Decimal Classification: Fic

Library of Congress Catalog Card Number 57-7541

Printed in the United States of America by the
Polygraphic Company of America, Inc.

ABNER'S CABIN

by

ALF EVERS

pictures by

LEONARD WEISGARD

THIS SPECIAL EDITION IS PUBLISHED BY ARRANGEMENT WITH
THE PUBLISHERS OF THE REGULAR EDITION
FRANKLIN WATTS, INC.
BY
E. M. HALE AND COMPANY
EAU CLAIRE, WISCONSIN

So away went Abner to get his wife and their four children to live with him in the little log cabin that stood all alone in the forest.

The very first thing that Mercy and John and Charles and Patience and Priscilla did after they had admired the cabin from outside was to admire it inside. When they did that Abner heard a squeaking, scratching noise. He stood off and looked at the cabin.

"Yup," he said, "just as I thought. My family's so big and the cabin's so little that the walls are bulging. But we'll have to make do till I get some fields made and some crops planted so's we can eat. Then I'll have time to make the cabin bigger."

So Abner cut more trees and made some fields. He planted corn and wheat and a dozen hills of beans.

Then he said, "The cabin has been bulging long enough. Now's the time to fix it."

So Abner made another room for the little cabin.

"It's still little," he told the children, "but now it seems to me it's only half as little as before."

Then Abner made a real fireplace and chimney out of clay and sticks. He made a floor of split logs. And then he made the most wonderful thing of all. He made a real window for the cabin. Of course there was no glass in the window. But it had a wooden shutter that you could open and close. Patience and Priscilla took turns opening and closing the shutter all day long before they got tired of it.

Every year after that Abner cut down more trees and made more fields. He built a log stable for his cows and oxen. On winter nights he and the boys split pieces of pine logs into shingles. When they had enough shingles they nailed them on the roof of the cabin so that it wouldn't leak.

Then Abner said, "Now my cabin is finished. I don't see how anybody could possibly want a finer little log cabin. It's the finest log cabin in the whole valley, even if it is the only one."

Then Abner stood off and admired the cabin until the sun went down and he couldn't see to admire it any more.

For years after that Abner and Mercy and their children lived in the cabin and they were happy most of the time. The children grew up and went away and got married and had children of their own. And Abner and Mercy grew older and older and older until at last they died.

Then a man named William and his wife named Sue and their children named Betsy, Jane, and Francis came to live in the little log cabin. But by that time it didn't stand all alone in the forest. There were other log cabins and many fields along the muddy road that went by.

When Sue first saw the cabin she made a face.

"Can't say I like that little log cabin," she said. "I'd ruther live in a house."

"Don't you worry, Sue," said William. "When I do what I aim to do to that little log cabin you won't know it. It'll be as pretty as a picture in a solid gold frame."

So William put real glass in the cabin windows. He made a new chimney out of red bricks. He covered the log walls of the cabin with smooth boards. Then he and Sue and the children stood off to admire it.

"That's not what I'd call a cabin any more," said William. "It's a little house."

Sue took a long breath and then she sighed.

"You're right, William," she said. "It *is* a house. And it's so pretty I don't think I'll ever get my fill of admiring it — not even if I live to be as old as Methusalem, and that's eight hundred and some years."

William and Sue and their children lived in the house for a long time and some days they were happy and some days they weren't. William grew fine crops on his fields and helped new settlers build houses. Sue helped the neighbors' wives when their babies were born because she believed in being neighborly. The children grew up day by day and at last they got married and went away. William and Sue grew older and older and older until at last they died.

Then a man named Gus and his wife named Elinor and their children Fred and Kate came to live in the house. By that time the forest was all gone as far as a man could see and there were plenty of houses up and down the road.

When Elinor first saw the house she threw up her hands. She made a sound that was half giggle and half squeal.

"If that isn't the plainest, homeliest little old house I ever saw," she said. "Why, it's the plainest house in the whole country!"

Gus looked up and down the road and, sure enough, he didn't see a plainer house anywhere.

"Give me time, Elinor," he said, "and I'll make that little house fancy as a wedding cake."

So Gus had a man come in and put a porch across the front of the house. The porch was made of pine boards with shapes of leaves and stars and flowers cut out of them. Along the edges of the roof the man nailed some boards sawed out to look like waves racing across the sea in a storm. He made a bay window at one end of the house. Then he painted the whole house white except where he painted it brown or green.

When everything was finished Gus and Elinor and their children stood across the street to admire their house. They all gave a gasp when they saw it standing there with the new paint shining like silk.

"Gus," Elinor said, "I don't see how a little house could well be made fancier no matter how hard a body might try. There's no room left on it to put anything else!"

And the whole family stood there and admired their house until their eyes ached.

For years Gus worked in the flour mill down the valley. Every election day he helped count the votes. Elinor taught in the little new Sunday school on the other side of the village, and she made nearly all the children's clothes herself.

Gus and Elinor had their happy times and some that weren't so happy. Finally the day came when the children grew up and got married and went to live a mile or two up the valley. Gus and Elinor grew older and older and older and finally they died.

Then a man named Percy and his wife named Mabel and their son named Erwin came to live in the house. By then it stood on a regular village street with the houses pretty close together and little lawns and gardens between them.

Percy and Mabel took the porch off the front of the house and put a big window there instead. They put in a bell that went ting-a-ling every time anybody opened the front door. They filled the big window with jars of candy and cans of corn and peas and tomatoes because they were planning to open a tiny grocery store.

One afternoon Percy and Mabel and Erwin stood on the sidewalk and admired the store because it was all ready to open.

"Outside of New York or Chicago," said Percy proudly, "I doubt if there's a little grocery store anywhere in the country that's got the class this one has."

He and Mabel and Erwin stood there admiring their store until the sight of all that food in the window made them too hungry to admire anything but a good meal.

For a long time Percy and Mabel kept the store. Percy always dropped everything to give a hand when there was a fire in the village. Mabel visited neighbors when they were sick and brought them some of her homemade jelly to cheer them up. Sometimes Percy and Mabel were happy, sometimes they weren't. And other times they weren't sure which.

When Erwin grew up he married a girl in the next village and went to live there. Percy and Mabel grew older and older and older and the time came when they died.

Then a man named Joe bought the house. By that time there was a hardware shop and a tailor shop on the street and people said there would be a butcher shop any minute.

One morning Joe went to the house and stood there on the sidewalk looking at it. And he thought, "I'm going to get plenty busy here next week. I'll have my bulldozer push over that old shack. Then I'll put up a nice filling station. Red pumps with yellow trimmings. A man in a blue uniform to sell the gas. A big electric sign on top so that nobody can miss it."

Joe was so happy about what he was planning to do that he laughed right out loud.

Just then a man named Dick came along and asked Joe what he was laughing about. When Joe told him, Dick's face went all sad.

"Nossir," said Dick, "that's no shack you've got there. That's Abner's cabin — the oldest house in all Abnersville. It's a genuine log cabin all covered up with boards. I tell you people may not seem to care much about it, but they'll be plenty mad at you if you tear it down."

When Joe heard that he stopped laughing. He was planning to run for mayor that fall. He wanted everybody to like him.

"If that's the way it is, Dick, I'll wait," he said. "I'll think it over a week or two before I start anything."

While Joe was thinking it over, Dick got busy.

"Yessir," Dick told everybody he met, "Abner's cabin's coming down if we don't do something about it. Yessir, it's the oldest place in town. Wasn't another house in the whole blamed valley when Abner built it. Yessir, it's a genuine old-fashioned log cabin inside if you once got the stuff that's been put over it ripped off. Yessir, it oughta be saved and made into some kind of museum or something like that. That's what oughta be done, yessir!"

Plenty of people felt the way Dick did. Soon they were giving dimes and dollars and having food sales and band concerts to raise money for the "Save Abner's Cabin" fund. And by the time Joe had finished thinking things over he was talking just like Dick.

"What do you know," he'd say, "that little old house is a genuine log cabin! Oldest building in Abnersville, yessir. Would be a shame to tear it down. It oughta be a museum or something, that's what."

And a museum was what it became. First Joe, who had been elected mayor because of the fine way he'd pitched in to save the house, had a man who knew all about old houses come to town. And this man hired workmen to tear away windows and doors and the roof and floors until nothing was left but the parts of the house Abner had built long ago. Then the men put in logs and other things to take the place of those that were missing or worn out. They made the house look just as it had on the day that Abner finished it.

While this was going on the people of Abnersville were busy, too. They rummaged in their attics and cellars to find things that had belonged to Abner and his family and to the other people who had lived in the house.

When the cabin was all ready Mayor Joe declared a holiday. He called it Abner's Cabin Day. The schools were closed, the village band played its loudest, and there was a fine parade down Main Street and on to the cabin. Joe made a speech and opened the little cabin to everybody for the first time.

Thousands of people came to look at Abner's cabin. Inside they saw a fireplace just like the one Abner had made of clay and sticks, with Mercy's big brass kettle hanging in it. They saw Abner's Bible lying on the table he'd made with no tool but his sharp ax. They saw Priscilla's wedding dress hanging on the wall.

In the cabin's other room the people looked at pictures of William and Sue and Gus and Elinor and Percy and Mabel, and of the cabin when they had lived in it. They saw things that had belonged to all these families, and the things showed them how the people that came before them had lived and thought and worked.

When the people came out of the cabin they were all a little excited the way people are when they've found out something important. What they had found out was that their town didn't just grow up all by itself. It had been slowly built by many people like Abner and Mercy and William and Sue and the rest of them. These people had built the town as they planted and harvested crops and built houses and sang songs and told stories around the fire. They had built it as they tended babies and helped neighbors and sewed and cleaned and did all the thousands of other things people do every day. The people coming out of Abner's cabin that day felt grateful to all those who had made their town with its streets and schools and its tree-shaded park. They felt grateful for the stories that had been handed down to them, and for the old custom of helping a neighbor.

Most of the people coming away from the cabin paused on the sidewalk and looked back at it. They looked at the gray log walls with the chinking showing between the logs, at the clay chimney, and the roof of hand-split shingles. They looked at the window with a shutter just like the one Patience and Priscilla had opened and closed all day long. They stood there and admired the cabin just as hard as they could admire. Even Abner — on that long ago day when he had finished the cabin that stood all alone in the forest — hadn't admired it more.

THE AUTHOR

For 25 years **Alf Evers** has been writing stories for young people of all ages. His books have been translated into many languages, including Persian and Turkish.

ABNER'S CABIN is particularly dear to Mr. Evers' heart because it grew out of his life-long passion for small towns and old houses. He grew up in a 250-year-old house that was full of reminders of the past. Today he lives in another old house in the Catskill Mountains. He takes an active part in the affairs of the small community, and is proud of his office as president of the local Historical Society.

THE ARTIST

Leonard Weisgard was born in New Haven, Connecticut. After a memorable trip to London, which he found "dreary, wet, and full of fog and prunes," he returned to America and school in New York. School held few joys for young Leonard. Upon graduating he entered Pratt Institute to study illustrating. He stayed there two years, then went his own way, sketching and developing his own style. He has illustrated more than fifty books for children, a few of them written by himself. Some of his books have been chosen the outstanding books of the year by the Graphic Arts Society. In 1947 he was awarded the Caldecott Medal.

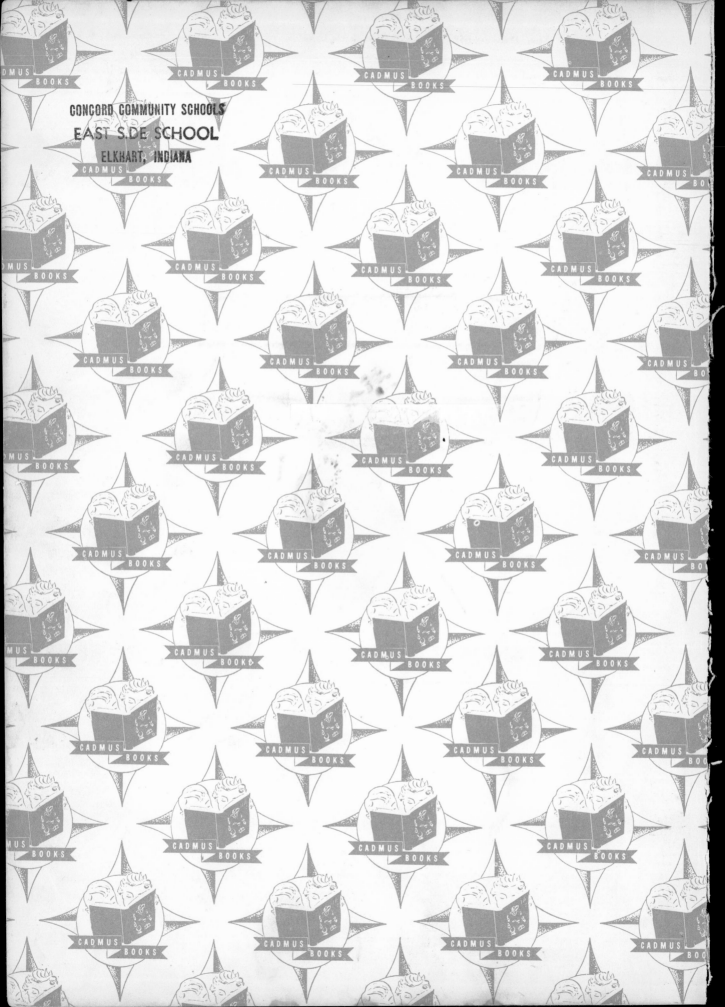